WITHDRAWN
WELLESLEY FREE LIBRARY

WELLESLEY FREE LIBRARY
WELLESLEY, MASS. 02482

Topic: Interpersonal Skills   **Subtopic:** Cooperation

Notes to Parents and Teachers:

As a child becomes more familiar reading books, it is important for him/her to rely on and use reading strategies more independently to help figure out words they do not know.

REMEMBER: PRAISE IS A GREAT MOTIVATOR!

Here are some praise points for beginning readers:

• I saw you get your mouth ready to say the first letter of that word.

• I like the way you used the picture to help you figure out that word.

• I noticed that you saw some sight words you knew how to read!

Book Ends for the Reader!

Here are some reminders before reading the text:

• Point to each word you read to make it match what you say.

• Use the picture for help.

• Look at and say the first letter sound of the word.

• Look for sight words that you know how to read in the story.

• Think about the story to see what word might make sense.

Words to Know Before You Read

big

build

hard

help

hill

scoops

shovels

small

DOZER
Builds A Hill
A Story About Teamwork

BY
KATY DUFFIELD

ILLUSTRATED BY
JOHN JOSEPH

Rourke
Educational Media

rourkeeducationalmedia.com

Dozer wants to build a hill.
He wants to build a BIG hill.

But building a BIG hill is hard.

Dozer pushes. He scrapes.

But the hill is still small.

"Maybe I can help," Backhoe says.

Backhoe shovels. He scoops.

Dozer and Backhoe work together.

PUSH!

SCRAPE!

10

SHOVEL!

SCOOP!

And the hill grows a little bit bigger.

"I want to build a BIG hill!" Dozer says. "Me, too!" Backhoe says.

"Maybe I can help," Dump Truck says. Dump Truck hauls. He dumps.

Dozer, Backhoe, and Dump Truck work together.

And the hill grows...

Big...

Bigger...

Biggest!

"That's a BIG hill!" Backhoe yells.
"It is!" Dump Truck says.

"We are a super-duper BIG hill building team!" Dozer says.

Book Ends for the Reader

I know...

1. What did Dozer want to build?

2. Who helps Dozer build?

3. What do Dozer, Backhoe, and Dump Truck call themselves?

I think ...

1. How can working as a team make a job easier?

2. Can you think of a time you used teamwork at home or school?

3. How can you work on something as part of a team today?

Book Ends for the Reader

What happened in this book?

Look at each picture and talk about what happened in the story.

About the Author

Katy Duffield is an author from Florida. Once, Katy got to run a dozer all by herself! She didn't build a hill, but she had lots of fun push-push-pushing the dirt around.

About the Illustrator

John Joseph's passion for art appeared at an early age, while living in Orlando, Florida. As a young boy, he was inspired by the many trips to visit the animation studios just down the road at the happiest place on Earth.

Library of Congress PCN Data

Dozer Builds A Hill (A Story About Teamwork) / Katy Duffield
(Let's Do It Together)
ISBN 978-1-64156-501-1 (hard cover)(alk. paper)
ISBN 978-1-64156-627-8 (soft cover)
ISBN 978-1-64156-737-4 (e-Book)
Library of Congress Control Number: 2018930717

Rourke Educational Media
Printed in the United States of America,
North Mankato, Minnesota

© 2019 Rourke Educational Media

All rights reserved. No part of this book may be reproduced or utilized in any form or by any means, electronic or mechanical including photocopying, recording, or by any information storage and retrieval system without permission in writing from the publisher.

www.rourkeeducationalmedia.com

Edited by: Keli Sipperley
Layout by: Corey Mills
Cover and interior illustrations by: John Joseph